T0197543

OH! THOSE CRAZY DOGS!

COLBY COMES HOME

CAL

Illustrated by: Rachael Plaquet

To order additional copies of this book, contact:
Xlibris
844-714-8691
www.Xlibris.com
Orders@Xlibris.com

ISBN:	Softcover	978-1-6641-8426-8
	Hardcover	978-1-6641-8427-5
	EBook	978-1-6641-8425-1

Library of Congress Control Number: 2021914104

Print information available on the last page

Rev. date: 07/19/2021

Introduction

This is a story about two crazy dogs, their adventures and the mischief they get into.

They are very loving dogs, but they can't help getting into things.

Hi! I'm Colby! I'm big and red and furry! I love everyone but sometimes people are afraid of me because I am so big!

Hi! I'm Teddi Bear! I'm big and white and very furry! I'm not as big as Colby, but just about. Everyone thinks I'm cute and I put shows on for them.

Our owners picked us out specially and brought us home to love and care for us. We love them too very much. They give us everything and a warm loving home. We will call them Mom and Pop

Sometimes, we don't listen to them, especially me, Teddi Bear!

But Mom and Pop love us anyway. Sometimes I get Colby in trouble. I can get him to do anything I want because he loves me too and can't say no. He protects me all the time.

COLBY GOING HOME!

One day, a man and a woman came into our pen at the kennel where we lived with our mother dog and my brothers and sisters.

It was a nice place, and we had fun running around together.

All my brothers and sisters ran to the edge of the pen wagging their tails and barking at the new visitors.

I stayed at the back of the pen and watched what was going on.

The lady looked at me and said, “I want that one,” pointing at me.

"He is so beautiful and the only red one." Our caretaker jumped into the pen and picked me up. He gave me to the lady.

She held me close and snuggled me right into her. She kissed me and talked to me and asked me if I wanted to go home with her. I barked a yes and wagged my tail. She laughed and said, "Oh yes, I will take him home."

The caretaker gave them some of my food and a toy and blanket just to get me comfortable until they could buy some new things for me.

My new mom held me all the way home, petting me and kissing the top of my head and talking softly to me.

She made me feel so loved and wanted. When we finally got to my new home, it was big and warm, and it had cats!

Oh boy! Something to play with! I went to chase one of the cats, and it turned toward me and puffed up his body and hissed at me with one of its paws raised up in the air. Wow! Did it have big claws!

The cat was bigger than me!

Okay, maybe I could find a smaller cat to chase. My new mom told me to leave the cats alone. For now, but I knew I was going to grow. They could probably hurt me a lot now. I left them alone for now and decided to explore my new home.

I went toward a room that smelled really good.

"Come with me" said mom, "you don't need to be in the kitchen right now!" Let me show you where you will stay most of the time. Mom picked me up and carried me up the stairs into a place she called a family room.

Wow was this nice! An awful lot better than my pen in my first home.

Wow! These must be the new toys Mom was talking about! All kinds of glittering balls and string and other things. Mom told me that I was not to touch the decorations. Aawww!

Mom picked me up and put me down into a large comfortable bed.

And when I looked up at her, she said, "You will be too big for this bed in no time." She put a soft toy puppy in the bed with me to keep me company. The toy puppy was bigger than I was.

Then I cuddled up with the toy puppy and had a long sleep because all the excitement made me tired.

When I woke up, I was excited and ready to play. I looked around, and suddenly, Pop came over and picked me up.

He said, "You probably have to go for a pee." He brought me to this area outside that was all fenced and put me down and said, "This is where you go pee." I stood there for a few minutes trying to figure out what he meant, but I had to pee so bad that I did. Pop clapped his hands and said, "Yay! Good boy, good boy!"

I was very happy that I had his approval and made him happy. I caught on to going to pee pretty quick because I liked it when I made them happy.

We went back upstairs to the family room, and I started to run all around the room and then I ran right under the Christmas tree.

"No!" Mom yelled. The Christmas tree was shaking and so was I.

Mom had never yelled at me before. I came out from under the tree very slowly, looking up at Mom.

Mom picked me up and cuddled me in her arms and told me that I wasn't to go near the Christmas tree. It was very special and could be knocked down very easily.

"No Christmas tree," she said. I gave a little bark and wagged my tail.

Mom smiled and put me down, and I ran right under the Christmas tree again!

Mom said "no" again. "You get out of there right now!"

Mom said, “You get out of there right now.”

I ran out from the other side and right into my bed.

Mom said, "Now you stay there!" She turned and went down the stairs, and I got up and followed her, happily wagging my tail.

Mom was going to the room that smelled so good.

Mom turned around to reach for something and tripped right over me.

"Oohh, Colby, are you all right?" She picked me up and held me. I was going to like living here. I got hugs for everything! I could tell she loved me, no matter what I did. What a great home! I think I'm going to stay here forever.

Oh, that crazy puppy!

Look for book 2, when Teddi Bear comes home!

Printed in the United States
by Baker & Taylor Publisher Services